First published in Great Britain in 2018 by Pat-a-Cake
This edition published 2019
ISBN: 978 1 52638 274 0 • 10 9 8 7 6 5 4 3 2 1
Pat-a-Cake, an imprint of Hachette Children's Group,
Part of Hodder & Stoughton Limited
Carmelite House, 50 Victoria Embankment, London EC4Y 0DZ
An Hachette UK Company
www.hachette.co.uk • www.hachettechildrens.co.uk
Printed in China

The Three Billy Goats Gruff

Retold by Ronne Randall
Illustrated by Richard Merritt

Little Billy
Goat Gruff

Middle Billy
Goat Gruff

Great Big Billy Goat Gruff

Troll

meadow

green grass

river

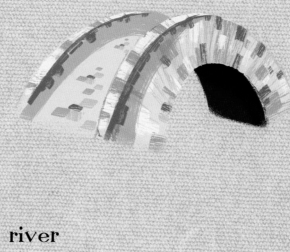

bridge

hillside

hooves

horns

splash

Once, high on a hillside, there lived three billy goats named Gruff. There was Little Billy Goat Gruff, Middle Billy Goat Gruff, and Great Big Billy Goat Gruff.

There was not much grass on the hillside.
But there was a meadow full of sweet
green grass across the river.

The three billy goats Gruff wanted to eat the sweet green grass!
To get to the meadow, they had to cross a bridge . . . but under the
bridge lived a great big, horrible troll.

Even so, Little Billy Goat Gruff decided to cross the bridge.
Trip-trap, trip-trap went his little hooves on the stone bridge.

Suddenly, with a thump and a bump, up popped the horrible troll!

"Who is trip-trapping across my bridge?" growled the troll.

"It's only me, Little Billy Goat Gruff," trembled the goat.

"I'm coming to gobble you up!" shouted the troll.

"Oh, please don't eat me," said Little Billy Goat Gruff. "I'm very little and very skinny! Wait for my brother, Middle Billy Goat Gruff. He is bigger than me and will make a much tastier meal."

So the troll let Little Billy Goat Gruff go, and he trip-trapped across the bridge to the green grassy meadow.

When Middle Billy Goat Gruff saw his brother eating the sweet green grass, he decided he would cross the bridge, too.

Trip-trap, trip-trap went his middle-sized hooves on the stone bridge.

Suddenly, with a crash and a smash, up jumped the horrible troll!

"Who is trip-trapping across my bridge?" he bellowed.

"It's me, Middle Billy Goat Gruff," said the goat.

"Ah ha!" cried the troll. "Your brother told me about you. I'm coming to gobble you up!"

"Don't bother eating me," said Middle Billy Goat Gruff. "Wait for my brother, Great Big Billy Goat Gruff. He is VERY big and VERY fat, and I'm sure he will be VERY tasty!"

"All right," snarled the troll. So Middle Billy Goat Gruff trip-trapped across the bridge to the green grassy meadow.

Then, along came Great Big Billy Goat Gruff. Trip-trap, trip-trap went his great big hooves on the stone bridge.

With a racket and rumble, a bang and a clang, up clambered the horrible troll.

"Who is trip-trapping across my bridge?" he roared.

"It's me, Great Big Billy Goat Gruff," said the goat.

"I'm coming to gobble you up!" shouted the troll.

"Oh, no, you're not!" said Great Big Billy Goat Gruff,
stamping his great big hooves.

He lowered his head, ran at the troll, and hit him with his great big horns.

SPLASH! The troll fell right into the river.

Then, Great Big Billy Goat Gruff went trip-trap, trip-trap across the bridge to join his brothers.

They munched, munched, munched the sweet green grass in the meadow, and they all grew big and fat and happy.

And no-one ever saw the big, horrible troll again!

Look at these two pictures. Can you see five things that are different in the second picture?

Help Little Billy Goat Gruff trip-trap his way to the meadow.
Mind the troll!

Meadow